KW-363-028

Have you got any ironing you'd like me to do?

Fatal Betrayal
and Other Stories

by

Carolyn Treavett

DORRANCE
PUBLISHING CO
EST. 1920
PITTSBURGH, PENNSYLVANIA 15238

The contents of this work, including, but not limited to, the accuracy of events, people, and places depicted; opinions expressed; permission to use previously published materials included; and any advice given or actions advocated are solely the responsibility of the author, who assumes all liability for said work and indemnifies the publisher against any claims stemming from publication of the work.

All Rights Reserved
Copyright © 2017 by Carolyn Treavett

No part of this book may be reproduced or transmitted, downloaded, distributed, reverse engineered, or stored in or introduced into any information storage and retrieval system, in any form or by any means, including photocopying and recording, whether electronic or mechanical, now known or hereinafter invented without permission in writing from the publisher.

Dorrance Publishing Co
585 Alpha Drive
Suite 103
Pittsburgh, PA 1523
Visit our website at *www.dorrancebookstore.com*

ISBN: 978-1-4809-2385-0
eISBN: 978-1-4809-2914-2

Fatal Betrayal

Rufus Renfrew, MP, was sitting in his comfortable flat, waiting for his friend Peter Bartholemew, another MP, to arrive. The flat was well furnished with a brown leather suite and thick pile cream carpet, but there were no excessive signs of luxury he could well have afforded. No pictures on the walls, which were white. His only indulgence was the drinks' cabinet, which he kept well stocked with alcohol. He walked across to it now and poured himself a generous measure of whisky from a cut-glass decanter. He was in his thirties and in a well-cut, grey three-piece suit he cut a tall, well-proportioned figure. He wasn't conventionally handsome but had a dynamic nervous energy, which made him attractive to women. With his bright red curly hair, he was noticeable and looked distinguished.

Big Ben struck eight o'clock, and there was a ring on the doorbell. Peter was always punctual. Rufus made his friend welcome and helped him to a glass of whisky. The two friends settled into an amicable exchange of greetings.

"I met a fantastic girl at a party last week," Rufus said. "She's got a wonderful body, beautiful upturned breasts. You'd love her, Pete."

"I'm a bottoms man myself," Peter said drily. "What about Pamela and the children?"

"Oh, they're buried in the deepest Cotswolds. She'll never find out."

"Who is this girl?" Peter asked.

"Annabelle."

"Annabel who?"

"You know. Annabelle the model. Her face is everywhere on posters advertising lipstick and such like. She's absolutely fabulous. I can't get enough of her."

"What on earth do you want with her?" Peter asked. "She's trouble. A vegan animal rights activist isn't the obvious choice for an MP from an agricultural constituency."

"Oh, I don't take any notice of that," Rufus replied nonchalantly.

"What about the Party? You'll never get a job in the Cabinet if this comes out."

"It won't come out. I'll see to that."

On Saturday, Annabelle was on a coach, taking a group of animal rights activists to a demonstration in Sussex to a farm that bred beagles for vivisection. Annabelle supported "Make Britain Cruelty Free," an organisation that campaigned against all forms of animal abuse, from homeless kittens to vivisection, from animals in circuses to factory farming. Annabelle was passionate about their causes, donated generously to their funds, and joined their demonstrations when she could. On the coach, she sat at the back between Colin Mathewson, the director of "Make Britain Cruelty Free," and another activist, Lance Fletcher, and they discussed the progress of the campaign.

Annabelle was not a classical beauty. Her mane of tawny hair was tended by a hairdresser in Mayfair. Her wide sensual mouth with her crooked nose made her unusual, but in photographs she appeared more attractive than she did in real life and the photographers clamoured for her. As for her affair with Rufus Renfrew, she kept it secret, not wishing to have her private life displayed in the press. He would visit her in her Chelsea flat and usually brought a bottle of champagne. She was able to compartmentalise her affairs. Once she had loved and it hadn't worked out, so now she realised that her affairs were not love but lust. Rufus Renfrew was good company and an amusing companion, but she didn't love him. She didn't go out to dinner with him, he being a meat eater, but preferred to dine alone or with Lance Fletcher, who would call for her at her flat and accompany her to a vegan restaurant in the King's Road, where they would discuss the progress of the campaigns and plans for new ones.

The coach reached its destination, and the occupants rushed out with banners and megaphones to surprise the owners of the farm. When they heard the commotion, the imprisoned dogs barked loudly, which made the demonstrators more determined.

Colin Mathewson addressed the demonstrators. "We're here to protest against the policy of the farm to breed beagles for vivisection. We are here to protect the innocent against the cruelty of big business, which breeds these dogs for profit. We have to stand up for justice, to protect the innocent against corruption. Let us all make our voices heard against this evil."

The demonstrators cheered and clapped and continued to wave their banners and to protest on their megaphones. In the evening paper that day was a photograph of Annabelle with the headline "Annabelle supports animal rights activists."

On Tuesday evening, back from their constituencies, Peter Bartholemew was pacing about in Rufus Renfrew's flat, trying to persuade Rufus that his association with Annabelle was detrimental to his political interests. But Rufus was not convinced and pooh-poohed Peter's arguments. Even when Peter showed him the photograph in Saturday's paper, Rufus was not convinced, saying that no one could connect him with Annabelle.

"She's given me a key to her flat," he said, "so I can slip in there unnoticed by the neighbours."

Peter became exasperated at Rufus's attitude. "You'll ruin your career chances associating with that troublemaker. It just isn't worth it," Peter said. "You'll have to give her up."

Rufus became angry. "You just don't understand, do you?" he exclaimed. "She's like a drug to me. I just can't do without her. So don't start lecturing me like this. The more I have of her, the more I need."

"You seem to have forgotten you're a married man with three children. If you don't care about your career, at least think of them. Think of Pamela and what it would do to her if she ever got to hear about it."

"I told you," Rufus said. "She hasn't got a clue. She trusts me, and the thought that I would be unfaithful just isn't on her radar."

"That makes it worse," Peter expostulated. "Haven't you got a conscience?"

"Sorry, Pete. We'll just have to differ about this. I know you're well meaning, but just drop it. There's a good chap."

Pamela Renfrew was content. She was happy with her life. She loved living in this big, roomy house in a picturesque Cotswold village. Her children were a joy to her. Rupert was four, Melissa was two, and Adam just one. She was a tall, elegant woman with dark hair cut into a neat bob. With her big dark eyes, she looked soulful and intelligent. She was sitting at the table in the large kitchen, sorting out recipes and putting them into some sort of order. For some time, she had toyed with the idea of writing a cookery book, having collected recipes from her mother and many friends. She enjoyed the garden of her house, and on this warm April day she took Adam in her arms and led the other two children out across the lawn. A magpie flew into the coppice at the end of the paddock, and a blackbird sang. The children's grey Shetland pony trotted up to her as she reached the fence. She fondled its nose and patted its neck. Then it trotted off again to join Rufus's chestnut gelding, which was cropping the grass at the far end of the paddock. They returned to the kitchen as Mrs Brown, who did the cleaning, arrived.

"They say it's going to be a fine summer," Mrs Brown said.

Pamela smiled. Mrs Brown was full of predictions, few of which ever materialised.

"I'll make a pot of tea," Mrs Brown said. "Then I'll get on with the bedrooms."

Pamela nodded and took the cup of tea that was offered to her. She felt that nothing could disturb the serenity of her life, and she looked forward with pleasure to the happiness ahead of her.

In the evening, after the children had been bathed and put to bed and after she had received a call from Rufus, Pamela poured herself a glass of red wine and settled down on the comfortable settee to listen to a CD of highlights from "La Traviata" in order to enjoy a relaxing end to her day.

Rufus Renfrew let himself into Annabelle's flat with a bottle of champagne under his arm. "Come on, Honky Tonk, get out the glasses," he said. "I want to talk to you."

Annabelle fetched a couple of glasses from her kitchen and set them on the coffee table before the blue velvet-covered settee. She was the kind of girl who collected soft toys, and everywhere there were ragdolls and teddy bears that she had received from friends and admirers.

"Now then," Rufus began, "do you have to go on so many demonstrations and get your photo all over the papers? You know you are making a lot of powerful enemies."

Annabelle looked rather puzzled and wrinkled her forehead. "I go on demonstrations because I believe in the cause. People should know what goes on behind the closed doors of laboratories and in slaughterhouses and on factory farms."

"Can't you just keep to your vegan diet and let that be enough? Do you have to shove it in people's faces all the time?"

"But I want to publicize the animal rights cause. I want people to know what goes on. I'm proud of being a vegan. No living thing has to die to keep me alive," she said passionately.

Rufus sighed. He wasn't getting through to her. "A lot of people make a lot of money from the things you demonstrate against. People are getting annoyed. I'm only warning you."

"Don't worry about me, Rufus. I have plenty of friends who are on my side. We have to change people's minds, and when they learn the truth things will change. You'll see."

Rufus looked into her young, open face and wondered how she could be so naïve. He wanted to protect her but realized there was nothing he could do; she was so determined in her opinions.

On Friday afternoon, Rufus Renfrew was speeding down the motorway in his BMW car on his way to the Cotswolds. On Saturday he would hold a surgery for his constituents, and on Sunday he proposed to exercise his horse. A few hours later, he turned into the driveway of his house and, clutching a bunch of red carnations for his wife, he entered the house. Pamela came to the front door to meet him, and as he presented her with the carnations he kissed her on the cheek and greeted the children, who came running to meet him, shouting, "Daddy, Daddy!"

That evening, while Rufus and Pamela were enjoying a meal of Beef Bourgignon, Pamela, looking puzzled, brought up the subject of "Make Britain Cruelty Free."

"A coachload of protesters came to Patrick Johnson's dairy farm on Wednesday," she said. "They were saying that the dairy industry is cruel to cows, and they gave out leaflets asking people to change to soya milk instead of cows' milk."

"Oh, don't take any notice of them" Rufus replied. "They're just a bunch of hotheads. Nothing to worry about"

"Well, Patrick Johnson was quite upset. He phoned me to tell me about it. I told him I would mention it to you. But I don't know that you'll be able to do anything about it."

"There's not a lot anybody can do. People have a right to peaceful protest, and as long as they don't break the law there's nothing that can be done to stop them."

Pamela sighed and went to the kitchen to prepare the coffee. It all seemed a far cry from the peaceful atmosphere that she was used to, but she felt sure that Rufus was right and she would put the demonstration out of her mind.

Peter Bartholomew was on his feet in the House of Commons at Prime Minister's Question Time. "When is the government going to take action against the activities of Make Britain Cruelty Free, an organisation that is campaigning to destroy Britain's pharmaceutical and agricultural industries?"

The minister replied that everything was being done to support the pharmaceutical and agricultural industries. Peter was concerned for his friend Rufus, and he had tried his best to warn him about the folly of his association with Annabelle, but Rufus didn't seem to take any notice, although secretly he himself was concerned for Annabelle.

On Tuesday evening, Rufus planned to surprise Annabelle and pay her a visit. He let himself into her flat, and the sight that greeted him shocked him. Annabelle was sprawled out on the floor of her sitting room, and there was a large wound on the back of her head. Her hair was matted with blood. Rufus stood, transfixed, not knowing what to do for the best. He took her wrist and found there was no pulse, so he got out his mobile phone and dialled 999 to report the death. Then he quickly let himself out of the flat and let himself into his own. He rang his friend Peter Bartholemew and asked him to come 'round as a matter of urgency. While he was waiting for Peter, Rufus helped himself to several generous portions of whisky, unable to control his thoughts. He had foreseen Annabelle would come to a bad end, but he still had not been prepared for the brutality he had witnessed. His hand was shaking as he opened the door for Peter.

"She's dead, Pete," he blurted out.

"Who's dead?"

"Annabelle, that's who. I found her just now."

Peter took the whisky that Rufus handed him. "What did you do when you found her?" Peter asked.

"Well, I dialled 999, then I left. Didn't want to get involved with the police, of course."

Peter looked thoughtful. "You may find you're implicated anyway. I told you to drop her, and now look what's happened. You could be in big trouble."

The following day, Rufus stayed in his flat, not feeling able to see anyone, but during the evening the doorbell rang and he opened the door to a weasel-faced woman with closely cut fair hair, accompanied by a middle-aged man. The woman flashed an identity badge at him.

"Detective Inspector Jeannette McKenna, CID," she said, "and Detective Sergeant John Baldwin," she added, indicating the man. "We'd like to ask you a few questions. Can we come in? I understand it was you who called 999 to report the death of Annabel Cross." The police-woman used the model's real name instead of her professional name "That's correct, isn't it?"

"Yes," Rufus managed to mutter.

"How well did you know the deceased?"

"Well, not all that well," Rufus prevaricated.

"But you were used to entering her flat? You must have known her quite well to do that."

Rufus remained silent. He felt trapped and didn't know how to get out.

"Were you sleeping with her?" Jeannette McKenna asked bluntly.

"Well, well, a few times."

"Come, come, Mr Renfrew, how long have you known her?"

"Well, for a few months, I suppose," Rufus replied unhappily.

"Were you acquainted with any of her associates?"

"No, none at all."

"We are treating as this death as murder, and we might need to question you again," Jeannette said, and they left.

Rufus was extremely worried about this turn of events and resorted to the drinks' cabinet for the rest of the evening.

The following day, the headline in the evening paper screamed: "MP quizzed in Annabelle death riddle." Rufus was alarmed and kept a low profile, not contacting anyone except Peter Bartholemew. Seeing his name in print told on Rufus's nerves, and he spent the evening with his drinks' cabinet, cursing himself for dialling 999 and giving the police a reason to question him. At least it was only the evening paper that reported the story, so it was unlikely that Pamela would hear of it. That was what he hoped until he went out the next day and found a group of journalists wanting to interview him.

"How did you find Annabelle, Mr Renfrew?" they asked. "What was your relationship with her?"

Rufus ignored,them just saying, "No comment."

Detective Inspector Jeannette McKenna and Detective Sergeant John Baldwin discussed the case at the police station. Jeannette McKenna despised women who made their living by their looks instead of their brains, so she had little sympathy for Annabel Cross, and Detective Sergeant John Baldwin, who was older than Jeannette, resented the fact that he had to answer to a woman—and a younger one than himself, at that—although he knew she had made her way in the force by grit and determination. They reviewed the evidence they had collected so far. They had the name of the director of "Make Britain Cruelty Free" and proposed to interview him that day.

When they reached Camden Town and located the small, dingy office where the organisation had its headquarters, Colin Mathewson was pleased to see them anxious to see justice done.

"Annabelle was one of our most important patrons," Colin said, "so I'll give you all the information you require so that the criminal who carried out this murder can be brought to justice."

"Can you give us the names and addresses of the people in your organisation who Annabel Cross associated with?" Jeannette asked.

Colin printed off a list from his computer. "They are very upset, understandably," he said.

Jeannette scanned the list. "We shan't need to interview the women," she said. "Such a vicious attack with a blunt instrument, probably a hammer, couldn't have been carried out by a woman; she wouldn't have been strong enough."

As they drove back to the police station, Jeannette looked through the names Colin had given them. There were a few married couples on the list, and Jeannette felt that it would be a waste of time questioning them. Detective Constable Mark Haynes had been dispatched to the block of flats where Annabelle lived to question her neighbours and had drawn a blank. None of them had ever spoken to her, and few of them had ever seen her. They had heard nothing suspicious on the day of her murder.

John Baldwin brought up the subject of Rufus Renfrew. "He's a tall, strong man who would have had the strength to carry out the attack, and he was the one to report the death," he said.

Jeannette was thoughtful. "We know he was having an affair with Annabel Cross, and we know that he is a married MP. If she became too demanding, for example, trying to persuade him to get a divorce, it's a possibility, I suppose. We'll have to question him again."

Rufus was alarmed to see all the coverage the murder got in the tabloid press in some of which his name was mentioned. He scoured the papers to see how many of the more serious ones dealt with the story. Pamela read the *Daily Telegraph*, and so far his name hadn't been mentioned in that paper, so he felt fairly safe—at the moment, at least.

During the evening, Jeannette McKenna and John Baldwin called at Rufus's flat for further questioning.

"What sort of relationship did you have with Annabel Cross, Mr Renfrew?" Jeannette asked.

"Oh, just a casual one," Rufus replied.

"Was there any reason you would have wanted Annabel Cross out of your life? For political or personal reasons?"

Rufus looked quite shocked. "Oh, don't think I'm the murderer. She was no problem at all to me."

The following day, Jeannette McKenna and John Baldwin went through the list that Colin Mathewson had given them.

"I think we should start out interviewing the men," Jeannette said.

So they went to Islington, where David Spencer lived. He proved to be a single man in his forties living in a bedsitter and was unemployed.

"How well did you know Annabel Cross?" Jeannette asked.

"Well, I saw her at demonstrations, but I've never spoken to her," David replied. "She was always with Colin or Lance Fletcher."

"Do you have any reason to believe that anyone would have done her harm?"

"Well, nobody in Make Britain Cruelty Free, of course. Of that I'm sure. She was a well-loved patron."

When Jeannette and John left David Spencer, they sat in their car for a while, considering what they had heard.

"I think we should see Lance Fletcher. He seems to have been close to Annabel Cross, and we may learn something," said Jeannette.

So they drove to Brixton and found a big imposing house, which had been divided into flats. They rang on Lance Fletcher's bell but got no answer. They knocked on the doors of some of the neighbours and were told that Lance Fletcher had disappeared a few days ago and had left no forwarding address.

Pamela Renfrew was sitting at her kitchen table and was proposing to start to write the introduction of her cookery book while Mrs Brown was making a pot of tea. There was a knock on the front door, and Pamela went to answer it. There was a scruffy-looking man on the doorstep holding a portable tape recorder.

As she opened the door, he said, "How do you feel about your husband's affair with murdered model Annabelle, Mrs Renfrew?"

Pamela was nonplussed. "I don't know what you're talking about," she said.

"You mean to say you hadn't heard? Which newspapers do you read? The affair is all over the papers. I can't believe you haven't heard."

Pamela quickly slammed the door in the man's face and went back to the kitchen, white faced and shaking.

Mrs Brown looked up, having heard the conversation between Pamela and the journalist, and said, "I'm sorry you should hear about it in this way. I saw about it in the *Sun* a few days ago. I didn't say anything because I didn't want to upset you."

"Rufus is coming down tomorrow, and I'll have it out with him then," Pamela said quietly and went back to the introduction of her book, though her hands were trembling.

Jeannette McKenna and John Baldwin were back in the police station. Detective Constable Mark Haynes came in, looking pleased with himself.

"I think I've cracked the Annabelle death riddle," he said.

"What have you found out, Mark?" Jeannette asked.

"Well, it seems that Lance Fletcher was an alias he used while working for MI5 as an undercover agent, infiltrating Make Britain Cruelty Free to find out their plans, and see if they were likely to do anything illegal in the way of animal rights activism."

"So what's his real name?" asked John.

"Well, it seems he is really George Price, who left MI5 and started working for an extreme rightwing group called Britain Forward. If we can find him, I think there are questions he needs to answer."

"Good work, Mark," said Jeannette. "We'll get the force out on his tail. He shouldn't be too difficult to find."

When Rufus reached his home on Friday, he could tell, by the frosty reception he got from Pamela, that she had heard about his affair with Annabelle.

"How could you, Rufus?" she asked.

Rufus looked shamefaced. "It wasn't anything serious," he said.

"Not serious! You have an affair with a model and it isn't serious! And you were questioned about her death. Did the police suspect you?"

"No, not really. I was questioned a couple of times, but they didn't seem to doubt me when I said had nothing to do with her death."

"How could you, Rufus? Didn't you give a thought to me and the children?"

"Oh, Pamela, can you ever forgive me for what I've done?"

Pamela looked into his troubled face and felt again the love she had had for him. "You'll have to sleep in the spare room tonight. It will take me time to get over this."

The police hunt for George Price extended throughout the country. Airports and ports were watched, and a day later he was arrested by two plain-clothed policemen as he was about to board a ferry to Calais. He put up no struggle and admitted to the crime as he was arrested.

The New Shop

The Nuffield family had lived in their big Victorian house in a leafy West London street for twenty-five years. Edith Nuffield, who prided herself as a homemaker, had chosen the furnishings carefully from stores in Oxford Street and had created a comfortable environment for her family. She was a big robust woman with a florid face and permed iron grey hair. She cared little for her appearance and usually wore tweed skirts, cashmere sweaters, and no make-up. In her fifties now, she had taken up the hobby of breeding pedigree Chihuahua puppies from two tan long-haired bitches, Mexican Pepita and Mexican Dolores. Her husband, Gordon, conducted a thriving business in partnership with his old friend from public school, Victor Brunswick, a widower whose wife had been killed in a road accident five years ago. They had a chain of shops selling electronic goods, which made them a good income. Edith and Gordon had one son, Jonathan, who worked in the business. Edith's mother, Vera, had been moved into the flat at the top of the house since she had suffered problems with her heart and was now on heart stimulant medication.

On Saturday afternoon, Edith was visiting her mother in the flat, which was redolent with Vera's lavender eau de toilette. For as long as she could remember, her mother had used the same perfume and it had become part of her personality.

"I've brought your new prescription," Edith said.

"Put them in the cupboard in the bathroom," Vera replied.

"Do you feel these pills are doing you any good?" Edith asked.

"Oh, yes. My heart is much stronger since I've been taking them."

Whenever she got a new prescription for her mother, Edith would secrete a few of the pills into her own pocket, thinking to herself that you never knew when they would come in handy.

Then Vera asked, "Have you been to a dog show?"

"No, Mother, we haven't been to a dog show. I've been making marmalade all the morning, and I went shopping this afternoon and got your medication."

Edith was irritated by this question, which Vera asked periodically as though she still had a right to question her daughter's behaviour.

When she left the flat and went down to her own home, Edith encountered Mexican Pepita and Mexican Dolores creating a chorus of yapping.

"Your little monsters will never accept me, Ma," Jonathan said.

"Because you come here so seldom, they don't get a chance to get used to you. Will you stay for dinner?"

"No, sorry, Ma, I only popped in to see Dad and ask him about the new shop. Where is he?"

"He's out playing golf with Victor. How is Anthea?"

"I've finished with her, or rather she finished with me. I don't seem to have much luck with girls. I think I might be gay."

"Rubbish," his mother replied. "You're a businessman like your father. Businessmen aren't gay. Another one of your silly fads like the guitar lessons, which came to nothing."

"I was a teenager then," Jonathan protested.

"Well, you aren't much older now. You just haven't found the right girl. That's all it is."

Jonathan shrugged. "Will you try and find out about the new shop when Father comes home?"

"Won't you wait and speak to him yourself?"

"Sorry, Ma. Have to dash. I'm meeting Charlie at the pub at six." And he was gone.

As they walked around the course on this sunny April day, Victor and Gordon discussed the new shop they were planning to open and the question of who would manage it.

"We need someone solid," Victor said.

Gordon agreed.

"I've been thinking of Stanley. He's been with us some time and has proved reliable," Victor went on.

Victor was a tall thin man with bushy white hair and a bit of a stoop, and Gordon, who was shorter, seemed to be square. His head was square, and his stocky body seemed to be square. Since his wife had died, Victor had become more inward looking and less likely to rely on Gordon's opinions. Gordon said nothing, wanting to broach the subject of his own son but feeling that Victor would be unlikely to agree, and yet he and Edith had hopes that Jonathan would carry on the business, whereas Victor was childless.

Gordon said at last, "Jonathan is keen to progress."

Victor was silent, pursing his lips. "Wouldn't think he's had enough experience."

"But he's been working for us for five years now," Gordon pursued his case.

"Frankly, Gordon, old man, I don't want to be brutal, but I don't think Jonathan is mature enough to shoulder the responsibility. I don't think he has a head for business. Maybe in a few years' time," and he brushed off the subject.

They walked on in silence, each mulling over his own thoughts.

"Edith will be disappointed," Gordon said at last.

"Yes, I dare say, but Edith isn't involved in running the business. This is purely a financial consideration. We can't afford to take any passengers. We need someone solid, as I said before."

When Gordon came in, Mexican Pepita went up on her hind legs and waved her front paws in the air in a characteristic display of Chihuahua exuberance. He stroked the little dog's head and went upstairs to change. He came down dressed in casual grey slacks and a cream Aran sweater and sat down to the dinner Edith had prepared. While they were eating their beefsteaks, Edith broached the subject of the new shop.

"Jonathan was here this afternoon. He wanted to discuss the business of the new shop. Have you made up your mind yet?"

"It's a bit difficult," Gordon said. "I've discussed it with Victor, and he doesn't think Jonathan is ready for a managerial position."

"But he's been working for you for several years. When will he be ready?"

"Victor doesn't think Jonathan has a head for business, and I'm inclined to agree with him."

"But he's your son! If he doesn't get the chance now, when will he be ready?"

"He doesn't have enough experience."

"If he doesn't get the chance to be a manager, how will he ever get the experience?"

"I'm inclined to agree with Victor on this."

"Oh, Victor, Victor, Victor. It's always Victor you rely on instead of your own flesh and blood."

"Victor is a shrewd businessman, and I'm prepared to rely on his judgment."

Edith was disappointed. She had had ambitions for her son. She had wanted him to go to university, but Gordon had said that would be a waste of time and he would be better off employed in the business. She had wanted Jonathan to live at home, but he had wanted to be independent and Gordon had provided him with a flat. She sat down on the settee and Mexican Dolores jumped up beside her, rolled over on her back, and folded up her front paws. Edith obliged and rubbed the little dog's chest, and she closed her eyes in ecstasy. Edith looked around the room and took in the beige suite and the dark brown carpet and the pictures on the wall, all reproductions of Monet's *Waterlilies*. The room was relaxing. Hadn't she made a comfortable home for her family? But it didn't seem to be sufficient. What more could she do? Gordon, who was absorbed in his business, never seemed to notice her or take account of her desires. She felt her life had accounted for nothing. She wished she had had a daughter. If she had had a daughter, maybe she would have understood her and appreciated her. But instead she had had a son, an independent-minded son who seemed not to need her. She went over to the drinks' cabinet, took out a bottle of sherry, and poured herself a generous measure. She enjoyed the delicious taste the Amontillado sherry left lingering in her mouth every time she swallowed a sip. Indulging herself, she took several more glasses when her mother came down from the flat.

"I haven't got any hot water," Vera complained. "Can you come and look at the boiler for me?"

Edith sighed and followed her mother up to the flat. When they got there, Vera turned on her daughter.

"Have you been drinking?" she asked. "I can smell it."

"Just a glass of sherry," Edith replied.

She went into the kitchen and saw that the pilot light in the boiler was out. She relit it, and the boiler burst into life. Then Edith excused herself and went into the bathroom and closed the door. She went to the cupboard, took some more of Vera's pills, and put them in her pocket. She felt emboldened as an idea was forming in her mind.

"Down, little monsters, down," Jonathan joked as Mexican Pepita and Mexican Dolores expressed their displeasure at his arrival. He joined his mother in the kitchen, where she was drinking sherry. "I didn't expect to see you drinking on a Sunday afternoon."

Edith said nothing to that. "I wasn't expecting you to call," she slurred.

"Where's Dad?"

"Out playing golf with Victor, of course," his mother snapped irritably.

"Charlie's going on a gap year," Jonathan said. "His father's giving him the money. He's going to fly to Australia and then travel 'round the Far East. It should be a great trip."

Edith showed no interest in this and helped herself to more sherry.

Jonathan pushed back his floppy fair hair from his eyes. "I've been thinking. If Dad isn't going to let me manage the new shop, I might as well go with Charlie. I can't see much future for me in the business at the moment."

Edith pricked up her ears at this and looked alarmed. "You want to go so far away for so long?"

"Well, maybe Dad could let me have some money if he's not going to let me manage the shop."

"It's not your father who's opposed to you managing the shop. It's Victor. He seems to dominate your father now. I've tried talking to your father, but he seems to be completely under Victor's thumb."

"Well, I'll put the idea of a gap year to Dad. I really think it would be a great opportunity for me."

Edith was upset. "You can't just drop everything and go off to the other side of the world. What about your flat?"

"Oh, I can give that up," Jonathan said nonchalantly. "Without the business, I haven't got any ties here."

"But there's me and your father. We should miss you terribly."

The following Saturday, Edith was moving briskly 'round her kitchen, preparing the meal for dinner. Gordon had invited Victor to join them, and Edith had decided to cook Beef Wellington with zabaglione for dessert. She was a good cook, and she enjoyed having guests and entertaining them. When the food was ready and Victor had arrived, Gordon selected a bottle of Cabernet Sauvignon from his wine rack and opened it. As Victor didn't drink alcohol, Gordon poured out a glass of wine for himself and one for Edith.

When they were seated and were enjoying their meal, Gordon said, "Jonathan is talking about going on a trip with his friend for a year. They want to go to Australia and then travel 'round the Far East."

"That might be a good idea," Victor said, but Edith remained silent, holding in her desire to disagree.

"Edith isn't too keen for him to be away so long and so far away," Gordon said.

"Oh, I don't know. He's a young chap. It might do him good. Broaden his outlook," Victor responded.

'I know my opinion counts for nothing," Edith interjected at last. "I wanted him to go to university, but Gordon said he would be better off working in the business. Now after all these years, he's not experienced enough to manage the new shop. What is the future for Jonathan?"

Victor looked slightly embarrassed by Edith's blunt question. "Well, I'm sure after a while he'll be able to fit in. Maybe after this trip he's planning to take," Victor said, trying to be conciliatory. After they had finished the zabaglione, Victor smiled at Edith. "Another of your delicious meals, Edith," he said.

Edith smiled back. "Thank you, Victor. I'm glad you enjoyed it," she said and went out to the kitchen to prepare the coffee. When she came back, she handed a cup to Victor. "No sugar and no cream for you, isn't it, Victor?" she said, handing another cup to her husband and taking one for herself.

They were all drinking their coffee when suddenly Victor became breathless and convulsed, clutching his chest and falling backward off his chair.

Alarmed, Gordon leapt to his feet and loosened Victor's collar. "Victor's having a heart attack!" he said. "I'll go and phone Dr Phillips." And he went out to the hall, where the phone was.

Ignoring Victor, Edith swiftly collected up the coffee cups, took them to the kitchen, and washed them up, smiling inwardly and triumphantly to herself.

A Modern Medea

Claire had met Martin at her friend Marianne's party. Marianne's parties were famous among their group of friends and always went with a swing, and this was no exception. The sweet, sickly scent of marijuana pervaded the large room in this fashionable street in London's Notting Hill. The windows were open to the night air, which was warm and sultry, it being July. About twenty young people danced and talked in the dimly lit room. Most of them knew each other, but there were some strangers among them, which made for an interesting mix. You never knew who you would meet, and it was always interesting to meet new people. Claire had been chatting to Christopher, who was her Knight Errant, and was gazing at her with adoring spaniel eyes. They were sipping white wine. She was nineteen and strikingly beautiful, wearing a tight-fitting red dress, which flattered her figure and set off her dark curly shoulder-length hair. When she saw Martin come into the room, she immediately paid attention. He was tall and slim with a clean-cut profile and in his early twenties, dressed in jeans and a t-shirt. His brown hair was almost shoulder length and he was confident, knowing he was attractive to women.

Noticing Claire's large oblique brown eyes, he moved toward her but he didn't notice their coldness. "Why haven't I met you before?" he asked her and fixed her with a quizzical look, which she found attractive.

They were soon chatting and dancing to the hypnotic, pulsating beat of the music. After a while, when they were both exhausted with the dancing,

Martin took Claire's hand and suggested they sit down on the floor, and he produced a roll-up.

"Would you like a spliff?" he asked.

She took the joint willingly and inhaled deeply. They continued an animated conversation for the rest of the evening, and before they parted Martin took Claire's telephone number and said he would call her.

On the Sunday afternoon after the party, Marianne was visiting Claire in Claire's flat. They were in the sitting room, which was roomy and comfortable, and sunlight streamed in. Claire was stretched out on the red velvet sofa while Marianne sat in one of the matching armchairs. They were both sipping white wine and smoking and were talking about the events of the evening before.

"Who is Martin?" Claire asked her friend.

Marianne grinned. "Are you interested?" she asked, pushing her fingers through her short blonde curls. "He shares a flat with Michael. You know, who goes out with Angela. They couldn't come because they've gone to Paris for a week, so I asked Martin to come instead. He seemed to be quite interested in you."

Claire smiled. "He is quite tasty and took my telephone number and said he would call, but I don't know whether he will or if he's the type to forget," she said, and she shrugged.

"I don't know," said Marianne, "but keep your fingers crossed."

But Martin did phone, and he and Claire went out several times, enjoying each other's company. Martin had a good sense of humour, which Claire enjoyed, and they laughed and joked, finding each other amusing. Then they embarked on a tumultuous ffair. They were both young and found each other physically attractive, and Claire was unable to get enough of Martin. When they made love, she clawed his back with her fingernails and bit into his shoulder in the excruciating ecstasy of the orgasm.

"I love you!" she screamed and felt it should never end.

Martin moved into Claire's flat, and a year later the twins were born, a boy and a girl. They were Martin's pride and joy, and he paid them a lot of attention, spending as much time with them as he could. He marvelled at these tiny beings and was fascinated to examine their little fingers with perfect nails. When they gurgled at him and smiled, he was entranced. After they started to crawl around, Martin began to play with them, crawling around himself and encouraging them to follow him. It was not long before the twins started to toddle around and walk. This was a milestone in their development, which he rejoiced in.

They all lived together contentedly for a year or so, then Martin started spending nights away. He made lame excuses, and Claire became suspicious. Where was he going? Why didn't he want to spend the night with her?

"Where have you been?" she questioned him one night when he came in drunk.

"Never mind," he slurred. "I'll always come back to see you and the children," and he stumbled off to bed and fell asleep.

Their relationship became more and more strained. Claire was cold to Martin when he did come to play with the twins. Although Claire was interested in her children, she began to feel jealous of them, for she felt that Martin was more interested in spending time with them than he was in spending time with her. Martin appeared not to notice her coldness or he made no sign of noticing, and he didn't alter his erratic behaviour of turning up at odd hours of the night.

Then one day, he went away and didn't come back at all. Claire was distraught, pacing about in the flat, drinking wine and smoking. She phoned Christopher and asked him to come around. Christopher was a small man in his late twenties who wore glasses because he was shortsighted. His clothes were scruffy and he had tousled ginger hair and a pale complexion, but he adored Claire. He lived in his fantasies and dreamed of winning her, but his passion was not reciprocated. Claire was glad enough to put up with him because he was useful and was always willing to do her bidding.

"Martin has disappeared," she told him. "I haven't seen him for weeks."

Christopher was uncommunicative but eventually said, "Perhaps he won't come back."

"But he loves the children," she protested. "He said he would always come and see them."

Christopher didn't like being the purveyor of bad news to the girl he adored, and he stuttered nervously, "Haven't you heard the news?"

Claire wrinkled up her forehead with curiosity. "What news?" she asked, hoping for some gossip.

"Martin is living with Marianne now."

Claire was shocked and incensed. Her friend for so long had treated her shamefully, taking Martin away from her. Her sense of betrayal was complete.

Not only had Martin betrayed her but now Marianne, too. She felt cut to her very soul and completely helpless. She wanted to hurt them both in revenge for what they had done. She had visions of somehow getting a gun and shooting them both dead.

"How could she do this to me? She knew Martin was with me. How could she take him away from me?"

Christopher shrugged. "Just one of those things, I suppose," he said lamely. Then looking at Claire intently, he pleaded, "Why can't you love me? You know I've always had feelings for you. I would always be faithful to you. I would never treat you badly. I would never hurt you."

Claire sighed. "Oh, Chris, don't talk like that. You are like a brother to me. You know I'm fond of you as a friend, but it's not love. Not in the way you want. Life isn't as convenient as we should like it to be."

Christopher looked disappointed. He had declared his love for her to Claire many times, and he always hoped she would succumb eventually, but it hadn't happened.

Four weeks later, Martin phoned Claire. "I want to spend some time with the twins," he said. "I'll come and fetch them next Saturday afternoon about two o'clock."

Claire was furious. "You'll not take my children to see you with that woman!" she shouted.

"Come on, Claire. I never made any promises to you. Lighten up. I'm a free fellow."

Feeling hurt by Martin's callous attitude, all through that week Claire was nervous, feeling sick with distress and unable to eat. She was losing weight, and her hair was limp and unwashed. She called Christopher and asked him to come and see her.

"Martin says he is coming to take the children to see him on Saturday afternoon, but he'll never take them to Marianne's—I won't allow it," she said vehemently.

When Christopher saw her, he was alarmed to see the bad state she was in. She asked him to get some drugs for her, but he tried to persuade her to slow down with the drugs. They were obviously not doing her any good, and she was using far too many.

"Shouldn't you see a doctor?" he asked her, but as usual Claire took no notice of his advice.

On Friday she phoned him again. "Get me some hash, Chris, please," she pleaded.

Christopher came 'round to Claire's flat and reluctantly gave her the drugs she had asked for. She gave him the money she owed him and burst into tears.

Christopher looked into her gaunt, pale face, not knowing what to say. Then at last, he said, "But they're his children, too, so doesn't he have a right to see them?"

"Never, never!" she protested. "He'll never take them to Marianne's."

Christopher stumbled off, feeling worried. He didn't know what to do to help Claire in her predicament. It would be no good appealing to Martin because he was a man who cared little for the feelings of others so long as he got his own way, but Christopher really wanted to help Claire if he could, but he couldn't think of what he should do. He already felt it was too late now. He knew that Claire was a self-centred person who saw things only from her own point of view. Reluctantly Christopher stumbled away, back to his own flat.

Claire took the hashish, crumbled it up quickly with some tobacco, and made a joint. As she inhaled, her emotions were magnified. She staggered to the children's bedroom, where they were sleeping, and a coldness came over her. She went into her own bedroom and took up a pillow and, returning to the children, pressed it hard onto the face of each child, extinguishing their lives. She went to her own bedroom and threw herself onto the bed, sobbing and shaking. Her world had shattered like glass, and she didn't know what to do.

Claire awoke late on Saturday morning. She was dishevelled, not having changed into her nightclothes the night before. She went to the bathroom and splashed cold water onto her face, feeling dazed and disoriented. The weather was stormy, and thunder threatened. When the doorbell rang at two o'clock, Claire ignored it, knowing it would be Martin. The bell rang more persistently.

She went down to the door. "Go away!" she shouted. "Go away!"

"Claire, be reasonable and let me in."

She ignored him, but when he started kicking the door and shouting she was afraid he would break it down, and she reluctantly opened the door, looking at him venomously with dark eyes flashing.

"Where are the children?" he asked.

"Dead," she replied dully.

"Claire, what nonsense are you talking?"

"Go and see," she sobbed. "I told you you'd never take them to Marianne's."

Martin hurried into the flat, looking into all of the rooms, and when he went into the children's bedroom and saw the lifeless bodies of his children lying there, he broke down and sobbed.

"How could you do this?" he demanded of Claire, who had followed him into the room.

"I want you to suffer as you have made me suffer," she replied coldly. "You took my love and threw it away. It meant nothing to you. Now you'll know regret and suffering. This is my revenge."

She walked out of the room in a daze, and Martin decisively took out his mobile phone and dialled 999.

The Car Crash

Detective Inspector Charles Borrow sits at his desk, surveying the evidence. He is a big middle-aged man with greying bushy hair. A young woman's body is found by a dog walker in Mill Lane at 7.30 A.M. on a cold November day. She hasn't been interfered with sexually, and her handbag is beside her. There is no evidence that robbery is the motive. The murder weapon, a large knife, is still stuck in her back when she is found.

Gregory Parsons is happy on this mild, sunny September day because he is driving along in his old Ford car with the beautiful blonde Samantha beside him. He is twenty-five and has never had a girlfriend. For weeks he has been going into the Spinning Wheel Café, where Samantha works as a waitress, hoping to catch her attention. She is nineteen and has had many boyfriends, none of whom have lasted long. She sees in Gregory a man with a car with whom she can amuse herself for a while to liven up her dull life in this medium-sized Midlands town, where nothing ever happens.

Detective Inspector Charles Borrow calls in Detective Sergeant Ambrose Batchelor to discuss the murder case.

"What do we know about her?" Ambrose Batchelor, a tall, slim, well-dressed man, asks.

"Not a lot," says Charles Borrow. "There was a letter in her handbag addressed to Samantha Mayer, and there's an address on the housing estate. The first thing is to visit the address and see if that brings us anywhere nearer to solving this case."

So Detective Sergeant Ambrose Batchelor finds himself interviewing Iris Mayer, who is the victim's mother. She is a plump woman with stringy bleached hair in a grey jersey tracksuit who is sitting in front of the TV with a can of beer in one hand and a cigarette in the other. She doesn't seem surprised or upset to learn that her daughter has been killed.

"She was always a bit wild," she says.

"Did she have a boyfriend?" the sergeant asks.

"Oh, yes, there were plenty," her mother replies with a laugh. "The last one was Peter Simmons, who works at a factory on the Industrial Estate," and she gives him the address.

The Detective Sergeant makes his way to the Industrial Estate to interview Peter Simmons, who is a young man with short hair and a pleasant smile, which soon disappears when Sergeant Batchelor asks him when he has last seen Samantha Mayer.

"It was a week ago. She chucked me," he says morosely.

"So you were angry with her?"

"I was upset," the young man replies.

"Do you know of any other boyfriends she might have had?" the sergeant asks.

"The only one she talked about was Gregory Parson, a right idiot according to her. She said she only went out with him because he had a car."

The sergeant decides to visit Gregory Parsons. When he gets to the house, he finds himself in a neat, tidy terraced house with rose bushes in the garden, and the door is opened by the mother, Doris Parsons, who is a big, well-dressed middle-aged woman. The sergeant asks where Gregory Parsons is.

"He's gone to sign on," she replies coldly.

'When did he last see Samantha Mayer?" the sergeant asks.

"Oh, he hasn't seen her since September," Doris Parsons replies.

When Ambrose Batchelor gets back to the station, he finds Charles Borrow has some more information. Detective Constable Christine Taylor has been doing some research on the computer and has found out that Samantha Mayer was involved in a traffic accident in October. She had been driving a car without a licence and had driven into a set of traffic lights when they turned red. The owner of the car was Gregory Parsons.

"I think it's time to interview Gregory Parsons," Charles Borrow says.

So Charles Borrow and Ambrose Batchelor go to the neat terraced house to see Gregory Parsons. What they find is a big, pusillanimous young man in jeans and a sweater who weeps when Samantha's name is mentioned.

"I love her," he says in explanation.

"But she crashed your car," says Charles Borrow, "and it was a write-off."

"She persuaded me to let her drive," says Gregory, "but I didn't know she didn't have a licence." He starts to weep again.

When they get back to the police station, they survey the evidence they have collected so far.

"We know that Samantha Mayer had a traffic accident in October with Gregory Parsons, but Gregory's mother says he hasn't seen her since September," says Charles Borrow. "I think we should interview the mother again," he says.

So the next day, the detectives go back to the terraced house and speak to Mrs Parsons again.

"Mrs Parsons, you told us that Gregory hadn't seen Samantha since September, but in October he was involved in a traffic accident when Samantha was driving his car."

Mrs Parsons looks flustered. "Oh, maybe I made a mistake," she says. "The car was a write-off, and Gregory lost his job at the warehouse because he couldn't get there without the car," she adds truculently.

The officers leave and decide that they will have to interview Gregory at the police station.

So on the following day, Gregory walks into the police station for interview.

"Now then," says Charles Borrow, "you were involved in a traffic accident when Samantha was driving your car without a licence. That's correct, isn't it?"

Gregory agrees.

"Then because your car was a write-off, you lost your job at the warehouse, didn't you?"

Gregory nods.

"So you can't be feeling very kindly toward Samantha," pursues Charles Borrow.

"I love her," Gregory whimpers.

"But you must have been feeling angry with her," Charles Borrow goes on.

Gregory continues to weep silently. Seeing that he won't get any sense out of Gregory, Charles Borrow closes the interview. He calls in Ambrose Batchelor to discuss the case.

"Mill Lane is a shortcut to the housing estate," Charles Borrow says, "so she was probably on her way home. There are no prints on the knife, so the killer must have worn gloves. The knife itself is probably a kitchen knife. Gregory's behaviour doesn't seem to indicate that he would be capable of killing her. But it must have been a strong person to have stuck the knife in her back. What impression did you get of Peter Simmons? Is it worth bringing him in for further questioning?"

Ambrose answers that Peter Simmons seems to be an honest young man and he doesn't think it is worth calling him into the station. "He seemed puzzled to learn of Samantha's death and was a bit upset," he says.

Charles Borrow purses his lips and is thoughtful, thinking about the problem. "I still think the answer lies with Gregory Parsons," he says. "But how we are going to get any sense out of him, I don't know. Let's call him back again."

So the next day, once again Gregory shuffles into the police station for another interview. He sits hunched up and uncommunicative.

"Now Gregory, you must realise murder is a very serious business, so it's up to you to cooperate," Charles Borrow commences the questioning. "When did you last see Samantha?"

Gregory looks sorrowful. "After she smashed my car, she said she didn't want to see me again," he says mournfully.

"So that must have been in October."

Gregory nods.

There's a knock on the door, and Detective Constable Christine Taylor comes in to say, "Mrs Parsons wants to see Detective Inspector Borrow." He asks for her to be brought in.

Mrs Parsons seems to be in an excited state. Her hair is dishevelled, and her face is red. "You've got to let my Gregory go," she demands. "He wouldn't kill a fly. He's been in such a state since you've been questioning him. He can't sleep, and he's crying all the time. I curse the day he met that girl."

"Now then, Mrs Parsons," says Charles Borrow, "we are looking for a killer, and we want evidence. If you have any further information about the case, we'd be pleased to hear it."

She stands erect and, raising her voice, she shouts, "It wasn't Gregory! It was me! She was a wicked, evil girl. One evening I came back from my sister's, and she was in bed with Gregory. She was disgusting and immoral. She has ruined my Gregory's life, and I couldn't stand to see him so upset."

Charles Borrow looks at the distressed woman. "You'll have to make a statement, Mrs Parsons," he says.

She collapses into a chair and starts sobbing.

After Gregory is sent away and Mrs Parsons has made her statement, Charles Borrow and Ambrose Batchelor are enjoying a pint in their local.

"Well, I'm glad it's all over," Charles says.

"There's no accounting for a mother's love for a son," Ambrose adds.

Under the Star Apple Tree

Lorna sat in the launderette, watching the sheets spin around. This was the event that took up her Saturday mornings now. She contemplated her life, and the drudgery of domesticity was getting her down. The monotony of her existence was paralysing. She tolerated a boring job in an office to maintain her existence, but she had wanted more. She had always wanted to write a novel. She had made several attempts but never got beyond the first couple of pages. She had read Simone de Beauvoir and imagined that if she could meet a man like Jean-Paul Sartre, an intelligent man who could support her ambition, she would be able to write.

When the sheets were dry, she trudged back to the flat in Earl's Court. She wondered what Philip would cook for lunch. It was no mystery—it would be rice again, and she was sick of rice. But it hadn't always been like this. Lorna had met Philip one sunny day last July in Kew Gardens. She loved this place. The beautiful trees took her back to her childhood in the country. She was in the humid greenhouse, which housed the tropical plants, and was looking at a banana plant when Philip spoke to her.

"It takes a lot of work to cultivate bananas," he said.

She turned to look at him, a youngish West Indian man, smartly dressed and with a pleasant smile. She smiled back. "You know about bananas?" she asked.

"I grew up with them in Jamaica," he told her.

They continued walking around the greenhouse together. Then they went out into the hot sun and sat under a tree in the shade.

"I'm a country boy," Philip had said.

"I too love the country," Lorna replied.

They continued chatting amicably for some time, and when they both decided to leave Philip had invited her back to his flat in Earl's Court. He made some tea and she took in the neat, clean flat in which she sat. The furniture wasn't new but it was well cared for, and the blue carpet was clean. He was an electrician and obviously hard working.

"Do you like music?" he asked, and she nodded.

He put on a record of a gospel singer she had never heard of: Sister Rosetta Tharpe. She knew of Mahalia Jackson, but this singer was new to her and the pure, soulful music went straight to her heart.

"I like reading, too," said Philip. "At the moment, I'm reading a Chinese novel, *The Dream of Red Mansions*. It's a classic of Chinese literature. My father was Chinese," he explained.

When she looked into his face, she could detect oriental features about his eyes, and she could see that the Chinese blood had refined the Negro in him.

As she went back to her bedsitter in South Kensington, Lorna felt an elation she hadn't known before. Here was an intelligent, sensitive man. Wasn't that what she had wanted for so long?

After she had been visiting Philip for some time, he said to her one day, "I want someone to look after me. Do you want the job?"

Lorna had thought for a while. Simone de Beauvoir and Jean-Paul Sartre had never lived together but had occupied rooms in different hotels. But there again, she had told herself she wasn't Simone de Beauvoir and had decided to move in with Philip.

"I've always been interested in politics," he had said.

Lorna had always thought she should be interested in politics, too, but she knew little about it. Still, she felt she could learn by some sort of osmosis from this knowledgeable man.

Philip told her about the men who came to his father's shop in the evenings to drink rum and talk. "Outside the shop, there was a star apple tree, and they used to hold political meetings under it," he said.

Lorna became enthralled by Philip's conversation. He could talk all day long about life in Jamaica and never repeat himself. She felt this was a sign of great intellect. She said he should write down his memoirs and call it "Under the Star Apple Tree." He smiled and shrugged off her suggestion.

At Easter he played Handel's "Messiah," and although Lorna was familiar with the name of the music, she had never listened to it before and the richness of it seeped into her very soul. Lorna developed a love for Philip, which grew into a passion. She exulted in his beautiful golden-brown body. It was only through the intensity of the sex act that she could express her love for him. She never asked herself whether Philip loved her. It was enough that she adored him.

One day Philip looked at her strangely. "Are you pregnant?" he asked.

Lorna replied that she didn't think she was.

"Well, if you are, get rid of it," he said coldly.

His remark sent an icy blow to her heart like the thrust of a sharp knife, and after that there was a distance between them. Although Philip continued to cook the meals and bring back fruit— mangoes, peaches, and avocado pears—some of the joy seemed to drain from Lorna. She began to long for her own cooking, which Philip had never enjoyed. He had insisted on doing the cooking himself, as he always had.

One Saturday in May, when Lorna came back from the launderette, she noticed there was a letter for Philip, which had a Jamaican stamp on it. She wondered what it was and who it was from. She picked it up and took it into the flat. When Philip read it, his face took on a look of consternation and he quickly put it in the pocket of his denim shirt and said nothing. He was quiet for the rest of the day, saying little. Lorna could sense the strained atmosphere between them, and in the night when Philip was sleeping she, who was unable to sleep, got up, took the letter from the pocket of Philip's shirt, and read it at the window in the moonlight. "Darling Philip," it said, "I was so happy to receive your letter. It's been so long since we've been together, and I can hardly wait to see you again. You know you've always been in my heart and I have never loved another, only you. Yours, as ever, Geraldine."

Lorna folded the letter and put it back in the pocket, trembling. She felt coldness in her whole body, and instead of getting back into bed she dressed quickly, wiping the tears from her face, and collected her clothes and put them into her suitcase. Quietly she went out of the flat, into the cold night air. She made her way to South Kensington on foot in the dark and booked into a cheap hotel. There she threw herself onto the bed in the dingy bedroom and sobbed. All of her dreams had come to nothing, and the time with Philip had been nothing but an illusion.

The Pigeon Man

"Has Barbara come in yet?" Claude asked anxiously of Beryl, who was a seventy-year-old volunteer in this café run by a charity for the benefit of the homeless but was also frequented by the inhabitants of the local area, in a busy part of the King's Road in Chelsea, in a building that used to be a church. Beryl, who was a down-to-earth, practical woman, was amused by Claude, a man who was almost the same age as herself and a widower for many years, who had become besotted with an eighteen-year-old art student. One day he had told her he didn't like old women, and Beryl had smiled, thinking he was rather silly. He always wore a black beret and a black overcoat, seeming to pose as a French artist, and talking about his studio in the neighbourhood, although no one had ever seen any evidence of his artistic endeavours.

"I took her out for dinner yesterday evening. She was hungry, poor girl. She doesn't get much money, so I took her for a meal. Any man would be proud to be seen in a restaurant with a girl like Barbara."

Beryl, wanting to change the subject, asked, "How's Hector?"

"Oh, he's doing well. He'll soon be able to fly again."

Claude rescued sick and injured pigeons, nursing them back to health and later releasing them. He had picked up Hector, a bird with a broken wing, in Victoria Station. Claude had carefully bound the damaged wing to the bird's body with a bandage so that the bones could knit back together. He usually made his rounds where he could find vulnerable pigeons such as stations and squares and anywhere where food could be found, but since he had developed his interest in Barbara he had done less pigeon rescuing than usual.

The following day, Claude was back in the café, asking about Barbara. "I tried to ring her on her mobile phone," he said, "but I only got her answerphone, so I left a message and asked her to call me. But she didn't get back to me. I hope she's all right."

Beryl, who was washing up the plates and cups in the sink, was used to Claude's vagaries into fantasy concerning Barbara and said nothing.

"I'll have a cup of tea," he said, "and wait and see if Barbara comes in today."

But he waited in vain and eventually went back to his house and fed Hector.

Claude had seen Barbara in the distance several weeks ago, before he had had a chance to speak to her. She was a young woman with shoulder-length brown hair and a youthful figure who usually wore jeans and a sweatshirt, which were often splattered with paint. Her complexion was clear and delicate like a beautiful rose, Claude thought, and added to her attractiveness. He immediately became interested and made an effort to sit near to her and strike up a conversation. Being a beautiful girl, she wasn't at all shy or diffident, and they were able to converse about art, Barbara being an art student and Claude being an enthusiastic, though not very bold, amateur. He had made a point of waiting to see if she came in to the café and if so he would offer her a coffee, and thus a habit of meeting there arose. She found him quaint and rather other worldly and was amused by his courteous treatment of her as though she were a precious object to be cared for. Sometimes Barbara would come into the café with another girl, and on one such day she sat at Claude's table and introduced her friend.

"This is Katherine," she said, and Claude smiled at the dumpy blonde girl, who wasn't half as attractive as Barbara, offering to get both girls a drink.

When he got back to the table with the coffees, Claude was happy to enjoy the girls' animated conversation, not needing to join in. He was content to listen to their laughter and gossipy talk. He decided he liked the company of young people, which made him feel alive. He suggested they go to Hyde Park.

"We can walk to South Kensington and get the tube from there," he suggested. "By the time we get there, it will be time for lunch and we can have it in the café."

The girls readily agreed, and they made their way along the streets to South Kensington Station. As they walked, Claude pointed out things he thought the girls would be interested in. They were a cheerful bunch as they got on the tube at South Kensington Station. They travelled one stop to Hyde Park Corner, and Claude led the girls into the park. They wandered slowly through the park, admiring the trees and the signs of life bursting forth from them. Soon the trees would be in their full glory with new leaves. The squirrels were leaping about in the trees and spring was here, and Claude felt a resurgence of life.

When they reached the restaurant, they chose a table that would give them a fine view and settled down to discuss the menu.

"I'll have a pizza," said Katherine, and Barbara chose a baked potato with cheese.

Claude, unsure what to order, eventually decided on a baked potato with baked beans.

The tantalising aroma of the food reached their nostrils as it was brought to their table, and they all set about hungrily to devour it.

After they had had their meal, they wandered around the park and into Kensington Gardens, admiring the ducks and being amused by the children with kites and boats with remote controls on the pond. They were interested in the people who were exercising their dogs and admired the different breeds they saw. They all agreed that it had been a most enjoyable experience, and Claude felt enlivened and cheered by the company of the young people.

When he got home, Claude fed the pigeon that was in his kitchen and retired to his sitting room with its golden yellow distempered walls and the tasteful pictures displayed around the room. He went to the drinks' cabinet, poured himself a glass of sherry, and sat down on the beige sofa and, savouring the delicious taste of the sherry as he sipped it, he felt relaxed and content with his day. He was glad he had suggested the trip to the park and was sure the girls had enjoyed it, too. He switched on the television to settle down and watch the news.

The next day, he went to the café, hoping to see Barbara as usual, but she didn't come. Although he waited for most of the morning before deciding that she wasn't coming today and went back to his house, he felt a profound disappointment. The afternoon stretched out for Claude, and he decided to go to the supermarket to get a few things he would need for his supper. As he looked around for the things he needed, Claude couldn't help noticing the young women he encountered and decided none of them were as attractive as Barbara.

The following day, Barbara came into the café, accompanied by a young man.

"This is Neville," she said, introducing the young man. "He's on my course."

Claude felt an instinctive dislike of the young man. This tall, thin, gangling youth with the bad complexion and protruding ears was not good enough for Barbara, and he resented his presence when he had been hoping to have a conversation with her himself. As they were engrossed in their own conversation, Claude decided to leave the café and make his way home. He was quite upset at these developments and felt that the young man was an interloper in his private conversations with Barbara. He gave Hector some corn and ruminated about the day's events. Surely Barbara wasn't really interested in such an unattractive young man. He would go back to the café tomorrow and see what developed. Perhaps Neville wouldn't be there with Barbara. Perhaps it was just by chance that they were together today.

The next day, Neville came into the café alone and, spotting Claude, sat down at his table.

"Where's Barbara?" Claude asked.

Neville shrugged and said he was hoping to see her later on during the day. Unhappy about this, Claude quickly drank his tea and left. He decided to go to St James' Park and look for casualties among the flock of pigeons that congregated there. Walking around the park, ruminating about his feelings for Barbara, he tried to get his emotions in check, but he had become accustomed to having a cup of tea with her in the mornings and was unhappy at having that custom disrupted. He continued walking 'round the park and came upon a very young pigeon, which seemed to be in distress. It looked as if it was too young to eat the corn Claude threw down for it, so he picked it up and put it in the shopping bag he always carried with him for the purpose of transporting vulnerable birds with him back to his home.

When he got back to his house, Claude let himself in through the front door into the hallway, which was covered with a thick piled red carpet, which went up the stairs, and he went through to the kitchen. He looked at the young pigeon and decided to give it some liquid food. He made a mixture of a quarter of a Farley's rusk soaked in a drop of warm water, which he fed to the young bird with the aid of a dropper. Satisfied with his morning's work, Claude went out into his garden and did a bit of weeding, but he couldn't get Barbara out of his mind. The thought of his late wife usually came to him in moments of solitude, but now his mind seemed to be totally absorbed with thoughts about Barbara, which he found distressing.

The next day, Claude's phone rang and it was Barbara.

"Claude, can I see you this morning in the café, about eleven o'clock? There's something I want to discuss with you."

Claude was energized by her message and quickly washed and shaved and put on some aftershave and a clean shirt. He got to the café well before eleven, bought a cup of tea, and went and sat down at a table where he had a good view of the entrance so that he could see her as soon as Barbara arrived. Sure enough, at eleven-thirty she walked through the door, her long brown hair swinging as she walked. Her curvaceous figure, with the firm, bouncing, youthful breasts, which was revealed under a loose open brown coat and a pair of camel-coloured trousers, delighted Claude. He was pleased to see that she had changed out of her usual scruffy jeans and was looking very smart. He smiled a welcome to her as her sparkling eyes fell on his face. He bought her a cup of coffee, and she began at once.

"It's a very big favour," she said, opening her big blue eyes wide. Then she explained, "My father has sent me some money, but it's not enough to buy the car I want, and I was wondering if you could let me have £500."

Claude was not a poor man and he could easily give her the money, so although he hesitated at first, he knew he would give the girl the money she asked for. "Come with me to my house, and I'll write you a cheque," he said.

They walked together toward a road that led off from the King's Road and arrived at a neat white house with flowers in the front garden. He led her through the hallway. The house was always kept immaculate by the woman he employed to do the cleaning twice week. Claude made the way to the kitchen, where Hector was picking at some corn and, indicating a seat at the table, he invited Barbara to sit down. He opened a drawer in the table, got out his cheque book, and wrote the cheque.

"Why is that pigeon bandaged up?" Barbara enquired.

"He's got a broken wing."

"Is that bandage going to mend his wing?"

"Yes, he'll be able to fly in a short while."

"It doesn't seem worth the trouble," she said callously. "You might as well have left him to die. What does one more pigeon mean when there are so many?"

Claude was shocked by her unfeeling remark and said, "I like to help any creature in distress. After all, they are living things and deserve to be taken care of."

When she had the cheque in her pocket, Barbara said she had to rush off because she had to meet her mother for lunch.

Although he went to the cafe every day, Claude didn't see Barbara for some time. He missed her with her girlish giggles and humorous conversation until one day he was walking down the King's Road when a car horn tooted him. He looked 'round and there was Barbara, driving a little car with a young man beside her. She pulled up to the kerb, parked beside him, and opened the window, smiling at him.

"This is Geoffrey," she said, indicating the young man. "He's my fiance."

Claude congratulated them politely, but inside he was mortified and knew he wouldn't see Barbara again.

He bought a bunch of daffodils and took the bus on the long journey to the cemetery where his wife was buried. He walked slowly to the grave and, picking up the vase that was on it, he walked to the pump, where he was able to fill it up with water. Returning, he knelt down awkwardly beside the grave, as the arthritis in his right knee was painful, and he put the daffodils in the vase.

"Kate, Kate," he said in his mind to his wife. "Why did you have to die so young and leave me alone? I've been such a very, very foolish old man. Forgive me, my dear."

Wiping a tear from his eye, he got up and made his way back to the bus stop to go back to the city. As the bus travelled along the road, he was exhilarated by the sight of the fresh green young leaves on the hawthorn hedge beside it on this sunny April afternoon. The trees were coming back to life, too, and Claude felt rejuvenated himself.

When he got back to his house, Claude carefully took the bandage off Hector and, taking the bird into the garden, released him. He immediately flew up into the blue sky, free and strong. Claude watched him fly away, and he himself felt a release and a restoration of freedom. He felt he would not be troubled with thoughts of Barbara anymore.